NOT IN

By KEVIN LEWIS

Illustrated by DAVID ERCOLINI

ORCHARD BOOKS / NEW YORK

An Imprint of Scholastic Inc.

SIDE THIS HOUSE!

Once there was a curious boy
who did not care for game or toy
or any plaything
from a store.

He found them all,
block and doll,
every gadget,
truck, and ball,
to be a great big BORE.

Livingstone
lived to explore.

Every day he
searched, he spied
to see what could be
found outside.

And BUGS from leaf
and gale and tide
he brought
through his front door.

His wary mom?
She did implore…

"Livingstone Columbus Magellan Crouse,
I'll have no bugs inside this house!
I'll say it once. Won't say it twice.
To speak again will not suffice!"

So trying hard to keep his head,
he trapped a little MOUSE instead,
then hurried home to make its bed....

"Livingstone Columbus Magellan Crouse,
no mice allowed inside this house!
I've told you once. I've told you twice.
One more time, you'll pay the price!"

So smitten by its smell and charm,
he brought a PIG home from a farm
and wondered would it cause alarm....

"Livingstone Columbus Magellan Crouse,
why is that hog inside this house?
I told you twice! This time makes three!
Now get that thing away from me!"

So from within the forest's gloom,
he sneaked a MOOSE up to his room
and prayed this would not seal his doom…

"Livingstone Columbus Magellan Crouse,
is that a moose inside this house?
I warned you twice. Then once again!
This time makes four! When will this end?"

So feeling just a little zealous,
he sprung an ELEPHANT from the circus
and waited for a great big ruckus....

"Livingstone Columbus Magellan Crouse,
get that elephant out of this house!
I warned you twice. And then twice more!
This time makes five! I'll take no more!"

Then ignoring his first notion
that this might cause quite a commotion,
he made a beeline for the ocean....

And while you may think this a tale
impossible in scope and scale,
he soon returned home with a WHALE....

"Livingstone Columbus Magellan Crouse,
a whale, a *whale*, inside the house?
First a bug and then a mouse
and then that hog inside my house…
Then came the moose. An elephant, too.
And now this whale! Oh, what to do?"

So Livingstone Columbus Magellan Crouse
took the whale and left the house.
And while his mom sighed with relief,
sure she was done with all the grief,
Livingstone Columbus Magellan Crouse
brought a bug into the house....

His mother thought. She made a shrug,
then gave her son a great big hug,
which meant that he could keep the bug.

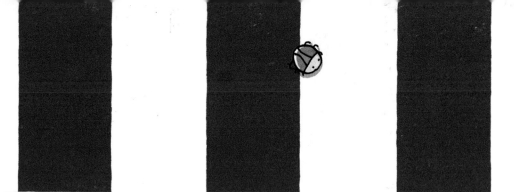

FOR PHIL, BECAUSE HE LIKES THIS ONE BEST.
— K.L.

FOR MY PARENTS.
— D.E.

With many thanks to Ken G., who started me on this journey, and to Elizabeth P., who never ceases to amaze.

Text copyright © 2011 by Kevin Lewis
Illustrations copyright © 2011 by David Ercolini

Library of Congress Cataloging-in-Publication Data Available
ISBN 978-0-439-43981-7

10 9 8 7 6 5 4 3 2 1   11 12 13 14 15

Printed in Singapore   46
First edition, August 2011
The artwork was created using ink drawing,
black-and-white painting, and Photoshop. The text was set in Times Roman.
Book design by Elizabeth B. Parisi